KV-678-786

KATIE WOO and PEDRO Mysteries

Mysteries

The Super-duper Supermoon Mystery

by Fran Manushkin

illustrated by Tammie Lyon

raintree
a Capstone company — publishers for children

Raintree is an imprint of Capstone Global Library Limited, a company incorporated in England and Wales having its registered office at 264 Banbury Road, Oxford, OX2 7DY – Registered company number: 6695582

www.raintree.co.uk
myorders@raintree.co.uk

Designed by Dina Her
Original illustrations © Capstone Global Library Limited 2023
Originated by Capstone Global Library Ltd

978 1 3982 4772 7 (hardback)
978 1 3982 4771 0 (paperback)

British Library Cataloguing in Publication Data
A full catalogue record for this book is available from the British Library.

Acknowledgements
Design elements by Shutterstock: Darcraft, Magnia

Printed and bound in India

Contents

Chapter 1

Camping out

Katie Woo and Pedro

were camping in the woods.

They ate tasty hot dogs and

toasted marshmallows.

Soon it got dark.

"Oh my," said Katie. "This dark is *very* dark!"

"Don't worry," said Katie's dad. "It won't last long."

"Why not?" asked Katie.

"It's a mystery," teased her dad.

"I love mysteries," said Pedro.

"Let's take a walk," said
Katie's dad. "Maybe we'll find
the answer to the mystery."

Whoooo! Whooo! Whooo!

A sound came from above.

"Yikes!" yelled Katie. "It's a
ghost!"

"No way!" said Pedro.

"That's an owl hooting on its

way home."

"Oh," said Katie. "Good!"

Crack! Crack! CRACK!

"Uh-oh," said Katie.

"What animal is making

that noise?"

"It's not an animal," said Katie's dad. "It's a branch breaking from a tree."

"Oh," said Katie. "Right."

Chapter 2

One mystery revealed

Katie and Pedro and her

dad walked a bit more.

Katie said, "You told me the dark is going to stop. I hope it's soon."

"I hope it's soon too," said Pedro. "And what about the mystery?"

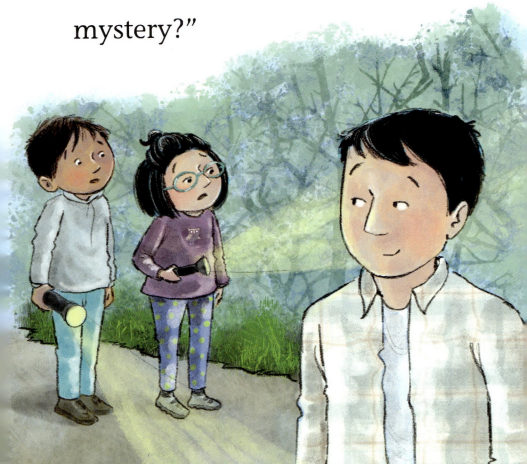

"Can you see something

bright up ahead?" asked

Katie's dad.

"I see the moon!" said Katie.

"That's the answer to the mystery," said Katie's dad.

"Of course," said Pedro. "The moon chases away the dark."

"That moon is so big!"
said Katie. "And so bright.
It looks so close I can almost
touch it."

"Right," said Katie's dad.
"Tonight, the full moon is the
closest it comes to Earth."

"We have a special name
for it," he said. "We call it a
supermoon."

"Wow!" said Katie. "That's
a super-duper name!"

Chapter 3

Another mystery!

"Let's head back to
camp," said Katie's dad.
"It's getting late!"

"Uh-oh!" warned Katie.

"I can hear footsteps. Maybe
it's a bear!"

But it wasn't a bear.

The super-duper full moon

lit up . . .

Katie's mum!

She told them, "I've been looking for you. I have a surprise."

"Another mystery," yelled Pedro. "Wowzee!"

"The mystery is a treat,"

said Katie's mum. "Cookies!"

Katie smiled. "There is no mystery about cookies: They are always super!"

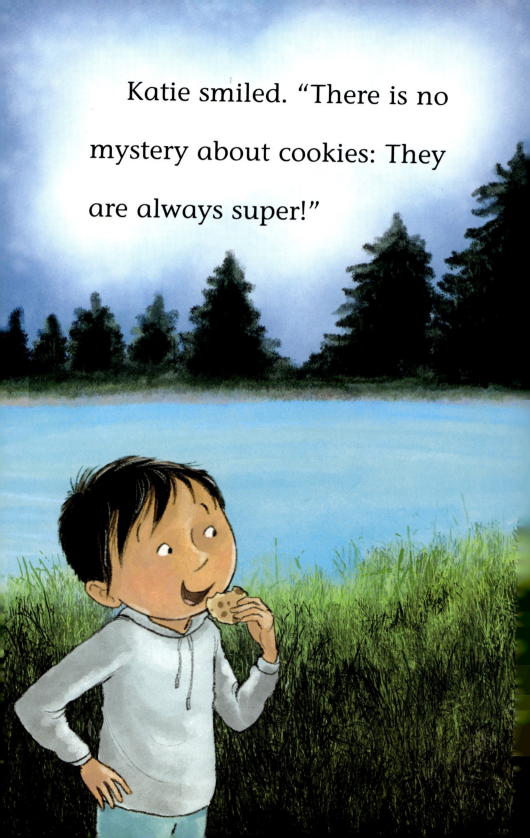

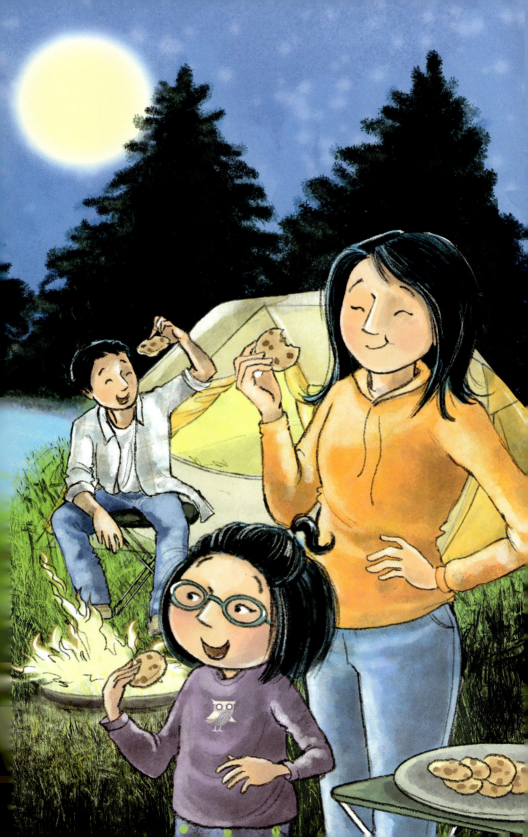

About the author

Fran Manushkin is the author of Katie Woo, the highly acclaimed fan-favourite early-reader series, as well as the popular Pedro series. Her other books include *Happy in Our Skin*, *Plenty of Hugs!*, *Baby, Come Out!* and the best-selling board books *Big Girl Panties* and *Big Boy Underpants*. There is a real Katie Woo: Fran's great-niece, but she doesn't get into as much trouble as the Katie in the books. Fran lives in New York, USA, three blocks from Central Park, where she can often be found bird-watching and daydreaming. She writes at her dining room table, without the help of her naughty cats, Goldy and Chaim.

About the illustrator

Tammie Lyon, the illustrator of the Katie Woo and Pedro series, says that these characters are two of her favourites. Tammie has illustrated work for Disney, Scholastic, Simon and Schuster, Penguin, HarperCollins and Amazon Publishing, to name a few. She is also an author/illustrator of her own stories. Her first picture book, *Olive and Snowflake*, was released to starred reviews from *Kirkus* and *School Library Journal*. Tammie lives in Ohio, USA, with her husband Lee and two dogs, Amos and Artie. She spends her days working in her home studio in the woods, surrounded by wildlife and, of course, two mostly-always-sleeping dogs.

Glossary

mystery puzzle or crime that needs to be solved

super-duper very wonderful

supermoon full moon that happens at the same time as when the Moon is closest to Earth. This makes the Moon look bigger and brighter than usual.

tasty when something tastes good

All about mysteries

A mystery is a story where the main characters must work out a puzzle or solve a crime. Let's think about *The Super-duper Supermoon Mystery*.

Plot

In a mystery, the plot focuses on solving a problem. What is the problem in this story?

Clues

To solve a mystery, readers should look for clues. What are some of the clues in this mystery?

Red herrings

Red herrings are bad clues. They do not help solve the mystery. Sometimes they even make the mystery harder to solve. What clues in this story were red herrings?

Thinking about the story

1. What were some of the typical camping activities Katie and Pedro did in the story? What other camping activities do you like to do?

2. The sounds she heard outside seemed to bother Katie. Why do you think that is?

3. Onomatopoeia is when a word sounds like the thing it is describing, for example "hiss". There are two examples of onomatopoeia in the story. What are they? Can you think of more examples of onomatopoeia?

4. Write your own story about a supermoon.

Make a light-up moon

Katie and Pedro were wowed by the super-duper supermoon. You can make your own super moon with this fun light-up project.

What you need:

- cup
- craft glue
- water
- paint brush
- balloon
- small bowl to put your balloon on
- toilet paper, torn into squares
- needle or scissors
- battery-operated tea light candle

What you do:

1. Using the paint brush, mix equal parts water and glue together in the cup.

2. Blow up and tie the balloon and balance it on the bowl so it is steady while you work.

3. With the paint brush, apply the glue mixture to the balloon in small sections. Cover the glue with a piece of toilet paper. Repeat this step until the entire balloon is covered, except the bottom. Let dry for about 5 hours.

4. Add a second layer of glue and toilet paper to the balloon.

5. Let dry overnight. When it is completely dry, pop the bottom of the balloon using a needle or scissors. Pull out the balloon pieces and throw them away.

6. Display your balloon over a battery-operated candle and watch it glow!

Solve more mysteries with Katie and Pedro!

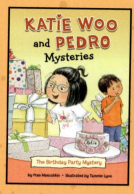

KATIE WOO and PEDRO Mysteries

The Birthday Party Mystery

by Fran Manushkin • illustrated by Tammie Lyon

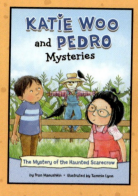

KATIE WOO and PEDRO Mysteries

The Mystery of the Haunted Scarecrow

by Fran Manushkin • illustrated by Tammie Lyon

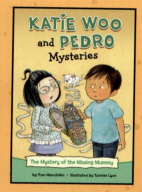

KATIE WOO and PEDRO Mysteries

The Mystery of the Missing Mummy

by Fran Manushkin • illustrated by Tammie Lyon

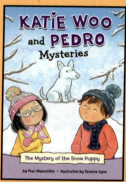

KATIE WOO and PEDRO Mysteries

The Mystery of the Snow Puppy

by Fran Manushkin • illustrated by Tammie Lyon

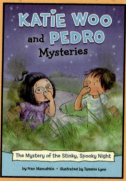

KATIE WOO and PEDRO Mysteries

The Mystery of the Stinky, Spooky Night

by Fran Manushkin • illustrated by Tammie Lyon

KATIE WOO and PEDRO Mysteries

The Peanut Butter and Jelly Mystery

by Fran Manushkin • illustrated by Tammie Lyon

KATIE WOO and PEDRO Mysteries

The Rainbow Mystery

by Fran Manushkin • illustrated by Tammie Lyon

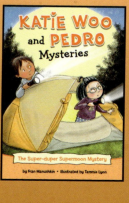

KATIE WOO and PEDRO Mysteries

The Super-duper Supermoon Mystery

by Fran Manushkin • illustrated by Tammie Lyon